# Buster and the Great Swamp

## by Marc Brown

**LITTLE, BROWN AND COMPANY**
New York ⋅ Boston

Copyright © 2005 by Marc Brown. All rights reserved.

Little, Brown and Company, Time Warner Book Group
1271 Avenue of the Americas, New York, NY 10020 • www.lb-kids.com
First Edition: September 2005
Library of Congress Cataloging-in-Publication Data
Brown, Marc Tolon.
Buster and the great swamp / Marc Brown.—1st ed.          p. cm.—(Postcards from Buster)
Summary: When his father takes him to visit the Louisiana bayou, Buster sends postcards to his friends back home telling about the Cajun language, learning to catch crabs, and keeping watch for a swamp monster.
ISBN 0-316-15912-3 (hc)— ISBN 0-316-00125-2 (pb)
[1. Bayous—Fiction. 2. Rabbits—Fiction. 3. Postcards—Fiction. 4. Louisiana—Fiction.]
I. Title. II. Series: Brown, Marc Tolon. Postcards from Buster. PZ7.B81618Bja 2005 [E]—dc2     2004018620

Printed in the United States of America •PHX • 10 9 8 7 6 5 4 3 2 1

All photos from *Postcards from Buster* courtesy of WGBH Boston and Cinar Productions, Inc. in association with Marc Brown Studios.

# Do you know what these words MEAN?

**alligator:** a reptile with a long head and a long tail that lives in rivers and swamps; can grow to be 18 feet long

**bait:** food put on a hook or in a trap, used to catch animals.

**bayou:** (BYE-yoo) a marshy area or swamp, particularly in the southern part of the U.S.

**buster crab:** a soft-shelled, female crab found in Louisiana

**Cajun:** (KAY-jun) a type of French language spoken by some people in Louisiana

**pirogue:** (pih-ROHG) a small wooden fishing boat used in shallow, swamp-like waters

## Louisiana

- The state bird of Louisiana is the pelican.

- The state reptile is the alligator.

- Louisiana was named after a French king, Louis XIV.

- In New Orleans, it is against the law to tie an alligator to a fire hydrant.

"Hey, Buster," said Arthur.
"Why are all your clothes for
this trip green and brown?"

"I'm visiting a bayou,"
Buster explained.
"And I don't want
the alligators to see me."

"This is a bayou," said Buster's father.
"It looks like a swamp."

Buster took a deep breath.
"It smells like one, too."

Dear Binky,

This would be a good place to film a scary movie.

We could call it THE RIVER OF NO RETURN.

Buster

Dear Francine,

We saw a log that looked
like an alligator —
or maybe it was
an alligator that looked
like a log.

I couldn't tell for sure.

Buster

Francine Frensky
Maple Drive Apt. 5
Elwood City, U

They stopped to watch some kids catching crabs in the water.

"What kind of crabs are they?" asked Buster.

"Buster crabs," said one of the boys.

"Really?" said Buster.
"*My* name is Buster."

"I'm Jude," said one boy.
"And this is Diego, Morgan,
Ulysses, Alexander, Andrea,
and Marcus."

"You see," he added,
"the crabs come in through here.
But then they can't get back out."

Dear Arthur,

I watched some kids catch crabs.

They use bait in a trap to do this.

The crabs are hungry, but not very smart.

Buster

"Can you catch
swamp monsters that way?"
Buster asked.
"I've heard they're
pretty smart. I wish
I could see one now."

Dear Muffy,

I wonder what kind of bait you use to catch a swamp monster.

I hope it's not Buster bait.

Buster

Muffy Crosswire
432 Valley View
Elwood City

"I can show you where
a swamp monster is," said Jude.
"We'll take the pirogue."

"The what?" asked Buster.

"It's a kind of boat,"
Ulysses explained.
"That's how we say it in Cajun."

Dear Brain,

There's a language down here called Cajun.

It's a lot like French.

It came to Louisiana when people moved here from Canada.

Buster

Alan "The Brain" Powers II
22 Oak Street
Elwood City

Buster kept a sharp lookout
in the pirogue.

"How will I know
a swamp monster
when I see one?" he asked.

"They look like big lizards,"
said Jude.
"They're really long
and have sharp teeth."

There was a splash nearby.

"What was that?" Buster asked.

He looked around carefully,
but he didn't see anything.

Dear Binky,

The bayou is filled with plants that boats can get stuck in.

The swamp monsters like it when that happens.

Buster

Later, Buster drove away
with his father.

"I wish we had seen
a swamp monster," said Buster.
"I know we were close."

Dear Muffy,

It's harder to find swamp monsters than I thought.

They're very good at hide-and-seek, especially the hide part.

Buster

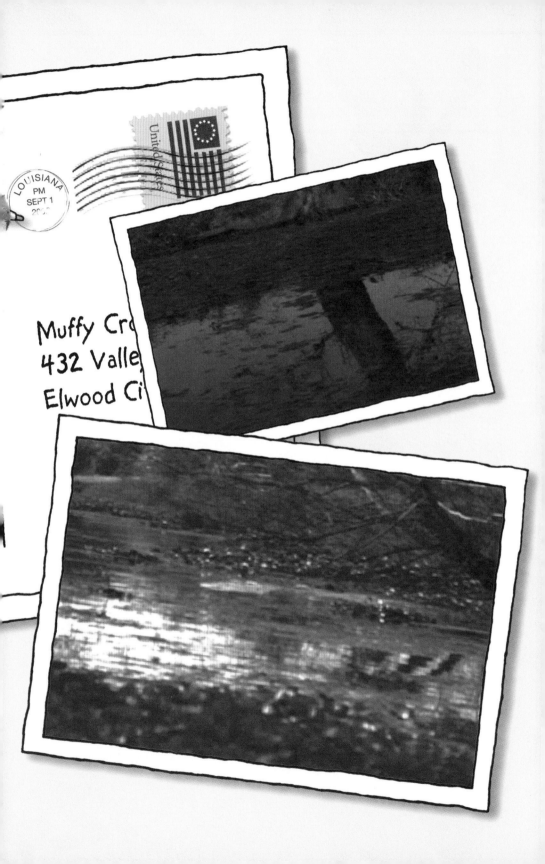

"Stop the car, Dad!" Buster shouted.
"It's a swamp monster!"

"Uh, Buster. . .I'm not so sure.
I think it's an alligator."

"Looks like a swamp monster
to me," Buster insisted.
"Wait until the gang hears
about this!"

Dear Everyone,

We don't have
any swamp monsters
up here, but I know there's
something living under my bed.

If I find it, I'll let you know.

Buster